Piggies

Dedicated to Marjane Wood

ISBN 0-590-50967-5

Text copyright © 1991 by Don and Audrey Wood.
Illustrations copyright © 1991 by Don Wood.
All rights reserved. Published by Scholastic Inc., 555 Broadway, New York, NY 10012, by arrangement with Harcourt, Brace & Company.

12 11 10 9 8 7 6 5 4 3 2   5 6 7 8 9/9 0/0

Printed in U.S.A.   08

First Scholastic printing, September 1995

Piggies

WRITTEN BY

DON AND AUDREY WOOD

ILLUSTRATED BY

DON WOOD

SCHOLASTIC INC.
New York Toronto London Auckland Sydney

I've got two

fat little piggies,

two smart

little piggies,

two   long

little piggies,

two silly

little piggies,

and two wee

little piggies.

Sometimes they're

hot little piggies,

and sometimes they're

cold little piggies.

Sometimes they're

clean little piggies,

and sometimes they're

dirty little piggies.

good little piggies,

but not at bedtime. That's when

they skip down my tummy,

dance on my toes,

then run away and hide.

So . . .

. . . I put them together, all in a row,

for two fat kisses,

two smart kisses,

two long kisses,

two silly kisses,

and two wee kisses goodnight.